For M.G.O.

The Dragon wore Pink

CHRISTOPHER HOPE

Illustrated by
ANGELA BARRETT

ATHENEUM · NEW YORK

The orphan egg lay in the forest. It was oddly shaped and faintly speckled, strangely pink and sadly small. Two enormous dragons watched it hatch. Grand Hector and Old Matronella stared at the small creature who showed his gums in a smile as bright as a pink chandelier.

In the misty past called the "Glorious Time", dragons were so mighty the maps of the world showed in a hundred places the warning:

HERE BE DRAGONS!

All that had changed. There were very few dragons left. They had forgotten how to fly and their wings had withered away. Their fires had grown cold. The maps no longer mentioned them. All they had left were their muscles.

It was to a dragon location on the edge of a dark plain, surrounded by thick forests stretching away to the peaks of faraway mountains, that Grand Hector and Old Matronella brought the orphan dragon. They called him Tarquin the Terrible because, as Old Matronella said, an orphan needs a good start in life and all they had to give him was a brave name.

However, everyone began to notice that Tarquin wasn't like other dragons.
Tarquin was odd.
He was fond of singing.
He smiled a lot.
And then there were the flowers.

When the first snowdrops appeared in the spring Tarquin stretched out full length on the ground and brought one eye, as big as a hot air balloon, right up against the tiny flowers.

Grand Hector taught him rearing, roaring and glaring – but Tarquin was hopeless. Then one day he was found with a bunch of bluebells behind his ear, admiring his reflection in a forest pool.

"Chinese dragons, paper dragons, perhaps even snapdragons! But a dragon with flowers behind his ear . . . never!" declared Grand Hector.

It was agreed that the sooner Tarquin was sent to work in the town the better.

He was given a large identity card on a chain to hang around his neck. It said:

TARQUIN, AGE 6,
WINGLESS WORKER DRAGON

"The town is miles away across the plain. It's surrounded by a wall we dragons built. The wall is to keep us inside during the day and outside at night," said Grand Hector.

"You will *hate* town," said Old Matronella.

But not a bit of it – Tarquin loved town.

But then one day he got on the bus and the driver chased him off: "Don't you see the sign?" he asked.

NO DRAGONS ALLOWED

He went into the shop. "Please leave," said the shopkeeper and pointed to the warning on the wall:

MONSTERS FORBIDDEN

He sat on a park bench. "Can't you read?" yelled the park keeper and pointed to the notice:

PEOPLE ONLY

Tarquin helped the grown-up dragons who hauled the logs, dug ditches, built roads, cleared the rubbish, and moved food from the storehouses and barns to the homes of the townspeople.

Older dragons sometimes became nurses to poor children and orphans.

One day as Tarquin was passing a park he heard someone crying and the sound of children singing. On a bench beside a pond sat a small, round girl with her fists to her eyes. Without hesitation Tarquin stepped over the wall and crept closer.

Ellie the Elephant.
She's so wild
Everyone knows!
She's a dragon child.

And the more the little girl wept, the more loudly the children chanted:

Ellie, Ellie, Rix Stix Stellie
She's so fat, she's so smelly –
Poor Old Elephant Ellie . . .

Tarquin's shadow fell chill on the backs of the children. The next moment a terrifying roar split the air. It hurt his throat but it worked. The children ran for their lives.

"Little girl," Tarquin asked in a hoarse whisper, "why are you crying?"

The girl lifted her face streaked with tears like raindrops across a window pane. "Because I'm fat," she said. "And my nose is too big. Look!"

Tarquin looked. "It suits your face, which is all you can ask of a nose, really."

"I remind people of things I'm not," said the little girl. "Mostly I remind them of an elephant."

Tarquin sat on the grass. "I know what you mean. I remind people of a dragon."

"But you *are* a dragon," said the little girl.

"My name is Tarquin the Terrible. But the others say I should be called Tarquin the not-terribly-good dragon."

"I like dragons," said the little girl. "When people get tired of calling me Ellie the Elephant, they call me the dragon child. I was raised by dragons, you see."

"Gracious," said Tarquin. "Your mother and father wouldn't have liked that."

Ellie didn't say anything. Tarquin suddenly understood.

"An orphan!" said Tarquin. "So am I. That means we're more in the same boat than ever. Shake friend!" Then he stretched out at Ellie's feet like a huge dog. "Would you mind climbing up and giving my back a good scratch?"

Ellie climbed onto Tarquin's back and gave him a good scratch. After a while she said in a rather quiet and especially ordinary sort of voice, "What are these little prickly things, Tarquin? Where your shoulder blades would be, if dragons had shoulder blades."

Tarquin thought very hard: "Would you say that these little things were at all pointy?"

Ellie said they were rather pointy.

"Besides being pointy, do they look to you in the least bit . . . wingy?"

Ellie said they looked distinctly wingy.

Then she said something even more surprising: "Did you know there was smoke coming out of your nose?"

She led him over to the pond.

Tarquin looked at his reflection. Trickling from his nostrils were two puffs of steel grey smoke. Very carefully he took a deep breath and blew it out through his nose. Ellie shrieked. Two jets of blue green flame hit the water with a smacking hiss and the pond vanished in a wisp of steam.

Tarquin put his head in his claws and sobbed great seagreen tears that filled the bone-dry pool in moments.

"Oh heavens, oh gosh, oh my! Whatever will Old Matronella say to me now? There never was a dragon more different from what a dragon ought to be."

"But Tarquin, you're what every dragon ever wanted to be; a real fire-breathing dragon!"

"Wanted to be – but isn't!" sobbed Tarquin.

Ellie had an idea. "Come home with me, Tarquin. I have a plan. Perhaps they don't have to know straight away."

Well, it's all very well suggesting that a dragon come home with you but you can't really hide a dragon, even a small dragon, behind an even smaller house without bits of him sticking out. It wasn't long before people noticed an ear, a claw, the end of a tail and put two and two together and came up with – a dragon!

Upstairs Ellie sat sewing Tarquin a shirt from the only things big enough – the sheets off her bed; large pink sheets which she stitched together, carefully cutting out holes for his head and arms. When she finished she wrapped the shirt in brown paper and tied up the parcel.

From her mantlepiece Ellie took a Japanese paper fan. Then she went downstairs to Tarquin. "This will hide your wings, for a while at least. Try breathing through your mouth and on no account sneeze! Keep this fan handy for any tell-tale clouds of smoke."

From the top of the town Ellie watched the young dragon making his way back to the dragon location across the now-darkening plain. She saw little bursts of flame every time Tarquin closed his mouth and breathed too fiercely through his nose.

Rumours began to spread that a whole gang of young dragons had been frightening children in the parks.

A crowd gathered outside Ellie's house. They threw things. They shouted: "Dragon child!" and "Ellie out!"

Soon there were search parties with flaming torches running here and there, charging after every shadow, shouting "Here's one!" and bumping into each other and falling over and scorching themselves. When they couldn't find any dragons they said that showed how clever the dragons were and how well they were hidden.

In the location Tarquin slept with his head on Ellie's parcel. At first light before any of the other dragons awoke he crept into the forest and there unpicked the careful knots with trembling claws. The pink shirt glowed in the sunshine.

A most shocking sight faced a party of dragons out for an early morning stroll. There was Tarquin, claw on his hip, fan at the ready, parading by the stream. A dragon wearing pink! Waving a fan! The dragons didn't stop running until they reached Old Matronella and Grand Hector.

"A pink shirt?" gasped Old Matronella.

"A fan!" bellowed Grand Hector.

It was the last straw.

"You're banished, Tarquin, from the dragon location. Find a cave in the faraway mountains and hide your terrible pinkness," said Old Matronella.

"And your fan," said Grand Hector.

The last the dragons saw of Tarquin was a small figure moving slowly across the dark plain. His pink shirt fluttered like a distant flag.

There were more shocks in store for the dragons when they arrived for work. Pinned on the gate was a large notice:

DRAGONS FORBIDDEN!

"How can you do without us?" Grand Hector shouted.

"We don't need you!" the people shouted back. "We can look after ourselves."

"Is that so?" the dragons shouted. "Well, we don't need you either."

This went on for at least half an hour until both sides were tired of it. The dragons returned to the location. The people went back to their houses. Just one small, rather plump girl with a notable nose was left standing on the wall. She was gazing across the plain hoping for a glimpse of pink. But of her friend Tarquin there was no sign.

Many miles away in a cave in the mountains Tarquin practised his fire breathing by drawing targets on the rock face.

And how he grew! The shirt which had once floated about him like a circus tent was now the size of a waistcoat on the mighty creature. The span of his wings threw great curling shadows behind him. He practised racing down the mountainside and taking off. He was learning again the art of flying which the dragons had forgotten.

There was just one problem. He hated looking down.

In the location things were not going well. The dragons were quite unable to grow their own food. They grew weak and faint. The townspeople were no better off without the dragons to work for them. The town became dirty, rubbish filled the squares and the food stayed in the barns and storehouses. People grew thin and ill. They looked for somebody to blame and found Ellie. If she loved dragons so much why didn't she go and live with them? With angry words they drove her from the town.

"But how shall I find my way?" Ellie cried. "Follow your nose!" came the cruel reply.

When at last Ellie arrived in the dragon location she asked for Tarquin.

"He covered his beautiful scales in a sort of sack. He began to look like a *person*!" Old Matronella shook her head sadly, "– like the people in the town, our bitter enemies."

"He dressed in pink," said Grand Hector. "Pink! So he's been banished to a cave in the mountains."

"But we're not your enemies," said Ellie. "Since the dragons left our town is a sad place. Please, won't you come back?"

Now Old Matronella was surprised to hear this, but she was proud. She answered in just one word: "Never!"

Slowly Ellie turned and set off again, this time for the mountains and Tarquin. He wasn't hard to find. For one thing he kept singing and the echo could be heard for miles.

And he was colossal!

He listened quietly while Ellie told him the story. The next day Old Matronella was very surprised to find the little girl had returned.

"I carry a message from Tarquin."

"That is not a name I know," said Old Matronella.

"Tarquin the Terrible."

"I know of no Tarquin – terrible or otherwise."

Ellie pressed on bravely. "Tarquin says you must lead your dragons to the town. Then take up battle formation."

The words 'battle formation' gave Old Matronella a shiver of excitement she hadn't felt for centuries. But she was still suspicious. "And why should I do what you ask?"

Ellie was ready for this. Tarquin had told her what to say: "Because you will see the Glorious Time again." After that there was no more argument.

As dawn broke the following day an amazing sight met the sleepy gaze of the townspeople. The entire tribe of dragons was drawn up in battalions outside the wall. At their head was a little girl, a round little girl. What were the monsters planning? The people rubbed the sleep from their eyes, fearing the worst.

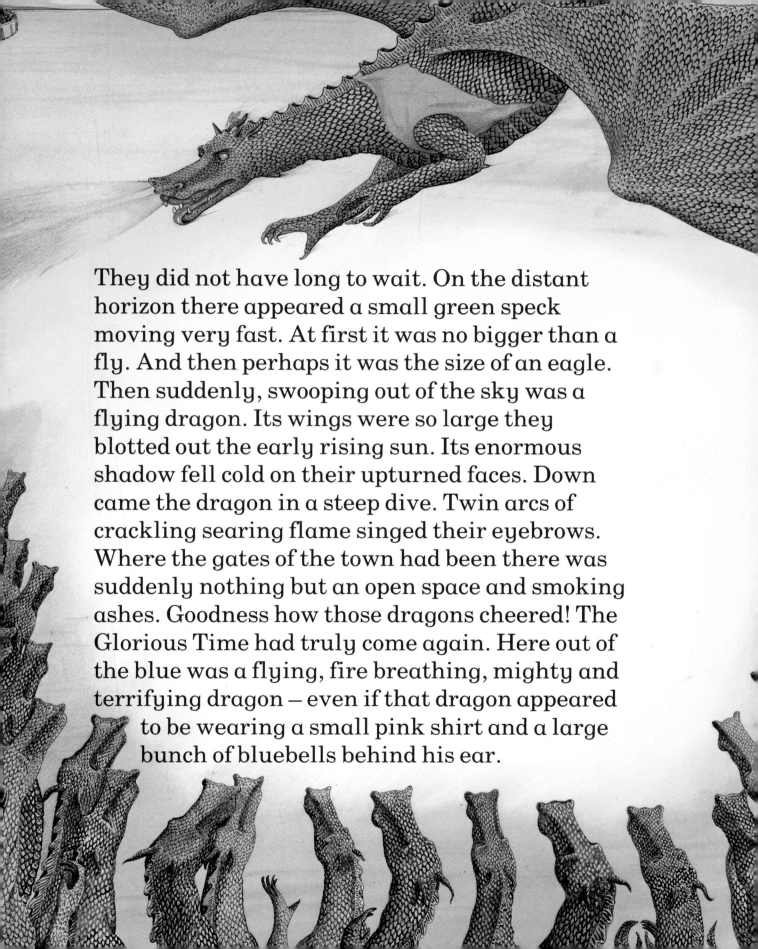

They did not have long to wait. On the distant horizon there appeared a small green speck moving very fast. At first it was no bigger than a fly. And then perhaps it was the size of an eagle. Then suddenly, swooping out of the sky was a flying dragon. Its wings were so large they blotted out the early rising sun. Its enormous shadow fell cold on their upturned faces. Down came the dragon in a steep dive. Twin arcs of crackling searing flame singed their eyebrows. Where the gates of the town had been there was suddenly nothing but an open space and smoking ashes. Goodness how those dragons cheered! The Glorious Time had truly come again. Here out of the blue was a flying, fire breathing, mighty and terrifying dragon — even if that dragon appeared to be wearing a small pink shirt and a large bunch of bluebells behind his ear.

Tarquin landed by the smoking gap in the wall where the gates had been. He held up a claw to quieten the cheering dragons.

"Remove the wall," he ordered.

The dragons were dumbfounded. Remove the wall?

"What dragons put up," said Tarquin, "dragons can knock down."

"We need the dragons just as much as they need us," Ellie told the townspeople.

So the town was repaired. All hateful signs were tossed onto a heap. Onto this great heap the dragons threw their identity cards. When night fell Tarquin set the great pile alight with a burst of flame. Around the huge bonfire people and dragons danced, singing and feasting until very late.

From that day on it seemed that dragons and people might live together as friends in the town without walls. And Tarquin the Terrible would keep things that way.

Well, that was the idea. And everyone thought it a very good idea — everyone except Tarquin. He preferred getting Ellie to teach him to sew. Then Ellie began to notice that he'd slip away when dragons and people came looking for him.

Ellie would have to say: "I'm sorry, but Tarquin's gone for a walk." Or "Tarquin's collecting flowers." Or "Tarquin is learning a very difficult cross-stitch and can't be disturbed."

"Dragons should never wear pink," Old Matronella declared. "It's a bad habit they picked up from people."

"We like dragons now, we really do," people said, "but we'd like them even more if they weren't so lazy and so slow and so big and so scaley."

All over the town the muttering grew worse. Tarquin spoke to Ellie: "If this quarrelling goes on, dragons and people will begin hating each other all over again."

Ellie sighed. "They need you to frighten them when they quarrel."

"I don't like frightening them."

The girl and the dragon looked at each other for a long time and knew they were both thinking the same thing.

"It's time we went," said Ellie.

"Shall we go far?" Tarquin asked. "I'm not very good at heights. I could make short local flights but if you're thinking of going somewhere overseas then I might have a problem."

"Leave that to me," said the ever-practical Ellie.

That evening she went to her sewing machine and made Tarquin a pair of blinkers of blue velvet, the sort that cart-horses used to wear, and attached these to a bridle of plaited leather and covered Tarquin's eyes.

"Now you can fly and I'll steer," said Ellie.

"Perfect," said Tarquin. "Where shall we go?"

"We'll just follow my nose," said Ellie.

They waited until midnight when people and dragons were fast asleep. Tarquin put on the blinkers and bridle and with Ellie firmly on his back they took off with a great surge of power from the dragon's wings.

"How does it look down there?" asked Tarquin.

"Peaceful," said Ellie, "very peaceful."

The wind rushed past her ears as they soared above the silent town.